THE TAROT JOURNEY

THE TAROT JOURNEY

AFFIRMATIONS, MINDFULNESS COLOURING AND SOUL JOURNALING WITH THE MAJOR ARCANA

The Sacred Space Press

The Sacred Space Press

THE TAROT JOURNEY

Affirmations, Mindfulness Colouring and Soul Journaling with the Major Arcana

ISBN 978-1-7640433-0-4

First Edition

Printed Worldwide

For more information, visit: thesacredspacepress.com

Cover and interior design by Abigail Henry

This book is dedicated to my soul connections - those whose love, wisdom and presence have shaped my journey in ways beyond words.

To my children, whose love and presence have shaped my soul and inspired me every day to grow, to love and to embrace the fullest expression of who I am.
Your light is my greatest joy and most precious gift.

To my husband, who walks beside me with strength and an open heart, through every challenge, every triumph and every chapter we write together.
Your unwavering support and deep love make this journey infinitely more beautiful.

This book is my way of honouring our journey.

About Me

My journey with divine energy has carried me across the world, yet one truth has remained unwavering: my deep love for healing, Tarot and guiding others toward self-discovery.

For decades, I have worked with Reiki healing, Tarot readings and energy clearing, helping people release emotional blocks and reconnect with their true selves. As a Reiki Master, Practitioner and Teacher, I have had the honour of mentoring others on their own spiritual paths, supporting them in finding balance, clarity and inner peace.

Tarot has been my trusted companion for over twenty years - offering insight, illumination and those gentle cosmic nudges that remind us we are always being guided.

My spiritual path is deeply woven with ancestral wisdom. My maternal grandmother read tea leaves, while my paternal grandfather practiced ancient folklore healing. Their gifts, stories and traditions have shaped my practice and inspired me to create this book as a bridge between Tarot's wisdom and your personal journey of transformation.

The Tarot Journey: Affirmations, Mindfulness Colouring and Soul Journaling with the Major Arcana is more than just a book - it is an invitation. An invitation to explore Tarot's wisdom, to reflect, to heal and to create. Through affirmations, mindfulness colouring and soul journaling, I hope to offer you a sacred space for self-discovery, growth and deep inner exploration along the way.

Wherever you are on your journey, know that you are not alone. I am honoured to walk this path with you. Let's embrace the wisdom of Tarot together.

With Love, Light & Laughter

Abigail

Your Journey Begins

1. The Enchanted Gateway
2. Self-Discovery with the Major Arcana
3. Transforming Through Tarot Wisdom
4. The Fool's Journey a Path of Growth
5. The Power of Tarot Affirmations
6. The Power of Mindfulness Colouring
7. The Power of Soul Journaling
8. Tarot Affirmations for Growth & Alignment
9. The Benefits of Tarot Affirmations & Soul Journaling
10. Steps to Effectively Practice Tarot Affirmations
11. A Journey of Affirmations Mindfulness Colourings & Soul Journaling for each Major Arcana:

    - The Fool (0)
    - The Magician (I)
    - The High Priestess (II)
    - The Empress (III)
    - The Emperor (IV)
    - The Hierophant (V)
    - The Lovers (VI)
    - The Chariot (VII)
    - Strength (VIII)
    - The Hermit (IX)
    - Wheel of Fortune (X)
    - Justice (XI)
    - The Hanged Man (XII)
    - Death (XIII)
    - Temperance (XIV)
    - The Devil (XV)
    - The Tower (XVI)
    - The Star (XVII)
    - The Moon (XVIII)
    - The Sun (XIX)
    - Judgement (XX)
    - The World (XXI)

12. Gratitude

The Enchanted Gateway

Tarot is more than just a deck of cards - it is a mirror to the soul, a guide through life's journey and a powerful tool for self-discovery. The Major Arcana represents The Fool's Journey, a path of transformation, challenges and enlightenment that mirrors our own personal evolution. Along this journey, we encounter lessons of growth, resilience and inner wisdom.

This multi-sensory workbook is designed to help you not only understand the Tarot but also live its wisdom through affirmations, mindfulness colouring and soul journaling. By engaging with each card's energy, you will cultivate deeper self-awareness, strengthen your intuition and align your mindset with your highest potential. Affirmations serve as a bridge between Tarot's guidance and personal empowerment, reinforcing positive beliefs and helping you step into your power.

Whether you are new to Tarot or have been working with the cards for years, *The Tarot Journey: Affirmations, Mindfulness Colouring and Soul Journaling with the Major Arcana* is an invitation to explore, reflect and transform. This is your sacred space to connect with Tarot, express your soul's truth and embrace the magic of your personal journey.

Let's begin - The Fool invites you to take your first step.

Self-Discovery with the Major Arcana

A Tarot deck consists of 78 cards in total, divided into two main sections: The Major Arcana (22 cards) and The Minor Arcana (56 cards).

Major Arcana - Represents the profound journey of the soul, mirroring the cycles of transformation, growth and self-realisation that we all experience. Each card holds a lesson, a moment of insight or a challenge that invites us to step further into our personal evolution. These twenty-two cards serve as spiritual milestones, marking significant turning points in our journey toward wisdom and enlightenment. While the Major Arcana focuses on life's bigger spiritual lessons and transformational experiences.

Minor Arcana - Reflects our day-to-day events, emotions and external influences. The Minor Arcana is further divided into four suits - Cups, Pentacles, Swords and Wands.

By focusing on the Major Arcana we are capturing the soul's journey, offering deep insights into personal transformation. The Major Arcana highlights life's defining moments - those pivotal shifts in perspective, growth and self-discovery.

Transforming with
Tarot Wisdom

From the innocence and boundless trust of The Fool to the wholeness and fulfilment of The World, the Major Arcana serves as a roadmap for personal and spiritual transformation. Each card represents a milestone in our evolution, guiding us through life's pivotal moments - whether they are new beginnings, challenges, revelations or triumphs.

As we progress through the Major Arcana, we are called to embrace change, release fear and trust in the unknown. The Magician teaches us to recognise our inner power, while The High Priestess urges us to listen to our intuition. The Tower may shake our foundations, yet it clears the way for new growth; and The Star reminds us to keep faith even in darkness. Each card holds a profound lesson, nudging us forward on our path toward self-awareness, resilience and enlightenment.

Through this journey, we are invited to step into our highest potential, learning not only to navigate life's ups and downs but also to transform challenges into opportunities for wisdom and empowerment.

THE FOOL'S JOURNEY

The Fool's Journey
a Path of Growth

The Fool's Journey is the story woven through the twenty-two Major Arcana Tarot cards, representing the journey of self-discovery, transformation and personal growth. It mirrors our own experiences, challenges and breakthroughs as we move through different stages of life. By understanding this journey, we can apply its lessons to bring more positivity, healing and wisdom into our everyday lives.

The journey begins with The Fool (0), who represents new beginnings, urging us to embrace opportunities with trust and curiosity. As we move forward, The Magician (1) reminds us of our power to manifest and create, while The High Priestess (2) teaches us to trust our intuition. The Empress (3) and The Emperor (4) highlight the importance of nurturing creativity and establishing stability in our lives. The Hierophant (5) encourages us to seek wisdom and spiritual guidance and The Lovers (6) helps us align with our values and relationships.

Progressing through the journey, The Chariot (7) empowers us with determination and Strength (8) teaches us resilience and inner power. The Hermit (9) calls us to reflect inward, while The Wheel of Fortune (10) reminds us of life's ever-changing cycles. Justice (11) urges us to seek truth and accountability; and The Hanged Man (12) asks us to see things from a new perspective. Transformation takes place with Death (13), guiding us through endings and new beginnings and Temperance (14) brings balance and harmony into our lives.

The Fool's Journey
a Path of Growth

As we continue, The Devil (15) challenges us to break free from limiting beliefs, while The Tower (16) forces sudden change for necessary growth. The Star (17) offers hope and renewal, The Moon (18) teaches us to trust the unknown and The Sun (19) illuminates our path with joy and success. Nearing completion, Judgement (20) calls us to embrace self-realisation and awaken to our true purpose, leading us to The World (21), where we achieve wholeness and fulfilment.

Each stage of The Fool's Journey offers wisdom that applies to our daily lives. Whether we are stepping into a new opportunity, overcoming personal struggles or experiencing transformation, the Tarot provides a roadmap for growth, healing and empowerment. By reflecting on where we are in our personal journey, we can shift our mindset, navigate challenges with greater clarity and embrace personal transformation.

The Tarot reminds us that every experience - whether joyful or challenging, is part of our spiritual evolution. As we journey through life, trusting the process, embracing the lessons and stepping into our highest potential allows us to live more consciously and with greater purpose.

The Power of
Tarot Affirmations

Affirmations

Affirmations are powerful tools for reprogramming the mind, shifting thought patterns and cultivating self-belief. When used consistently, they help replace negative or limiting beliefs with empowering statements that align with personal growth and transformation.

By integrating affirmations with Tarot, we can use the wisdom of the Major Arcana to reinforce positive changes in our mindset. For example, affirming "*I trust my intuition and inner wisdom*" when reflecting on The High Priestess allows us to embody her energy and strengthen our self-trust.

Practicing affirmations daily enhances self-awareness, reduces stress and helps manifest the life we desire by aligning our thoughts with our highest potential.

Mindfulness Colouring

Mindfulness colouring is a creative and meditative practice that promotes relaxation, focus and present-moment awareness. When combined with Tarot-inspired imagery, it becomes a profound tool for self-discovery.

As we colour, we engage both the logical and intuitive sides of our brain, allowing us to absorb the symbolism of the Major Arcana on a deeper level. The repetitive motion of colouring helps quiet mental chatter, reducing stress and anxiety while enhancing clarity and insight.

Colouring Tarot imagery mindfully also encourages us to connect with the lessons of each card in a gentle, non-verbal way, making it an excellent complement to journaling and affirmation work.

Soul Journaling

Soul journaling with the Major Arcana provides a structured yet intuitive way to explore personal growth, healing and transformation.

Each card in the Tarot tells a story, reflecting different aspects of our journey through life. When we write about our thoughts, emotions and experiences in relation to these cards, we gain valuable insights into our own patterns, strengths and areas for growth.

Journaling with Tarot allows us to engage with the archetypes on a personal level, helping us navigate challenges, clarify intentions and recognise the cycles of change we experience.

By incorporating prompts, affirmations, mindfulness colouring and soul journaling with the Major Arcana becomes a holistic practice that nurtures self-awareness, healing and spiritual empowerment.

Tarot Affirmations for Growth & Alignment

Blending affirmations with Tarot wisdom supports self-development, transformation and spiritual alignment. This practice helps internalise Tarot's lessons while reshaping thoughts, beliefs and actions to align with your highest self.

Rewires the Mind for Positive Thinking - Affirmations replace limiting beliefs with empowering thoughts. By affirming the wisdom of the Tarot, you begin to shift negative self-talk, creating new patterns of self-confidence and resilience.

Strengthens Intuition & Spiritual Connection - When you affirm the messages of a Tarot card, you deepen your understanding of its energy and connect more intuitively with its meaning. This practice strengthens your intuition and helps you receive clearer guidance.

Enhances Self-Discovery & Awareness - Soul journaling prompts you to explore how a Tarot card relates to your current experiences. Writing affirmations alongside your reflections encourages self-awareness and emotional growth, helping you integrate Tarot's wisdom into daily life.

The Benefits of Tarot Affirmations & Soul Journaling

Combining Tarot affirmations and soul journaling creates a powerful spiritual practice that deepens self-awareness, strengthens intuition and supports personal transformation. Each element plays a unique role in helping you connect with your higher self and navigate your life's journey with clarity and empowerment.

Cultivates Inner Peace & Emotional Healing - Affirmations help release past wounds, reduce anxiety and promote self-acceptance. When combined with mindful journaling, they become a tool for emotional healing and balance.

Supports Manifestation & Personal Growth - Affirmations help you align your energy with your goals and desires. By using affirmations inspired by the Major Arcana, you create intentional shifts in your mindset, attracting more of what you want into your life.

Deepens Mindfulness & Present-Moment Awareness - When paired with mindfulness colouring, affirmations allow you to fully immerse in the present moment, reducing stress and fostering a calm, centred state of mind.

Steps to Effectively Practice
Tarot Affirmations

These steps to effectively practice Tarot affirmations will support you in enriching your Tarot journey, strengthening your intuition and cultivating positive transformation by empowering you to elevate self-belief, reshape thought patterns and guide meaningful shifts along your spiritual path.

READ the affirmation with clear intention and mindful presence
- Find a quiet space where you can remain undisturbed and fully focused.
- Slowly read the words - aloud or silently - allowing their meaning to resonate within you.
- Connect with the energy behind the affirmation, rather than repeating it without thought.

Example: If the affirmation is "I trust my intuition", take a moment to reflect on where in your life you need more trust in yourself.

SPEAK the affirmation with confidence and heartfelt emotion
- Stand before a mirror, gaze into your eyes and declare the affirmation as though you already believe it to be true.
- Repeat it three to five times, allowing each word to carry conviction and uplifting energy.
- Notice the emotional shift within - let the affirmation echo through you and take root.
- If any doubts surface, gently acknowledge them but choose to return your focus to the empowering truth of the affirmation.

WRITE the affirmation in your soul journal to invite deeper reflection
- Write the affirmation several times to anchor its energy into your subconscious.
- Spend time with the mindfulness colouring page - allow the creative process to calm your mind and gently open your heart.
- Pause to connect with your emotions or sensations it evokes within you.
- Finally, allow the soul journaling prompts to guide you gently into a deeper inner journey.

Example: If the affirmation is "I am worthy of love and happiness", write about moments in your life where you have felt loved and explore ways to invite more of that energy in.

The Fool

A NEW BEGINNING, ADVENTURE, INNOCENCE
AND TRUST IN THE UNKNOWN

The cliff symbolises the unknown, the white dog signifies guidance and protection,
and the knapsack holds life's experiences.

I trust the universe and embrace new beginnings with an open heart

Soul Journaling

ALLOW YOUR SOUL TO SPEAK WITHOUT OVERTHINKING

➡ **WHAT EMOTIONS ARISE WHEN I CONNECT WITH THIS CARD?**
Reflect on the energy of the card and how it resonates with your current journey

➡ **HOW DOES THIS CARD'S MESSAGE APPLY TO MY LIFE TODAY?**
Explore how its wisdom can be integrated into your daily experience

➡ **WHAT ACTIONS CAN I TAKE TO EMBODY THE ENERGY OF THIS CARD?**
List steps that align with the lesson or insight provided

➡ **WHAT IS ONE AFFIRMATION I CAN CREATE FOR MYSELF BASED ON THIS CARD?**
Write your own empowering statement inspired by its meaning

➡ **CREATIVE EXPRESSION**
(Space for drawing, doodling or writing additional thoughts related to the card)

➡ **CLOSING INTENTION**
Write a short note of gratitude or intention for the day based on your reflections

➡ **THANK THE TAROT, YOUR HIGHER SELF & THE UNIVERSE FOR GUIDANCE**

The Magician

MANIFESTATION, PERSONAL POWER AND USING ONE'S TOOLS WISELY

The Magician connects heaven and earth, symbolising manifestation. The infinity sign represents limitless potential and the tools at his disposal - the Sword, Cup and Pentacle on the table and the Wand in his hand - symbolise mastery over the elements.

I have all the tools within me
to create the life I desire

Soul Journaling

ALLOW YOUR SOUL TO SPEAK WITHOUT OVERTHINKING

⇨ **WHAT EMOTIONS ARISE WHEN I CONNECT WITH THIS CARD?**
Reflect on the energy of the card and how it resonates with your current journey

⇨ **HOW DOES THIS CARD'S MESSAGE APPLY TO MY LIFE TODAY?**
Explore how its wisdom can be integrated into your daily experience

⇨ **WHAT ACTIONS CAN I TAKE TO EMBODY THE ENERGY OF THIS CARD?**
List steps that align with the lesson or insight provided

⇨ **WHAT IS ONE AFFIRMATION I CAN CREATE FOR MYSELF BASED ON THIS CARD?**
Write your own empowering statement inspired by its meaning

⇨ **CREATIVE EXPRESSION**
(Space for drawing, doodling or writing additional thoughts related to the card)

⇨ **CLOSING INTENTION**
Write a short note of gratitude or intention for the day based on your reflections

⇨ **THANK THE TAROT, YOUR HIGHER SELF & THE UNIVERSE FOR GUIDANCE**

The High Priestess

INTUITION, HIDDEN KNOWLEDGE AND SPIRITUAL WISDOM

The High Priestess sits between two pillars (Boaz & Jachin), representing duality. The scroll in her lap contains hidden knowledge and the moon symbolises intuition.

I trust my intuition and embrace my inner wisdom

Soul Journaling

ALLOW YOUR SOUL TO SPEAK WITHOUT OVERTHINKING

⇨ **WHAT EMOTIONS ARISE WHEN I CONNECT WITH THIS CARD?**
Reflect on the energy of the card and how it resonates with your current journey

⇨ **HOW DOES THIS CARD'S MESSAGE APPLY TO MY LIFE TODAY?**
Explore how its wisdom can be integrated into your daily experience

⇨ **WHAT ACTIONS CAN I TAKE TO EMBODY THE ENERGY OF THIS CARD?**
List steps that align with the lesson or insight provided

⇨ **WHAT IS ONE AFFIRMATION I CAN CREATE FOR MYSELF BASED ON THIS CARD?**
Write your own empowering statement inspired by its meaning

⇨ **CREATIVE EXPRESSION**
(Space for drawing, doodling or writing additional thoughts related to the card)

⇨ **CLOSING INTENTION**
Write a short note of gratitude or intention for the day based on your reflections

⇨ **THANK THE TAROT, YOUR HIGHER SELF & THE UNIVERSE FOR GUIDANCE**

The Empress

CREATIVITY, FERTILITY, ABUNDANCE
AND NURTURING ENERGY

The lush surroundings and wheat symbolise abundance, creativity and fertility.
She represents nurturing energy and the divine feminine.

I nurture myself and others with love, creativity and abundance

Soul Journaling

ALLOW YOUR SOUL TO SPEAK WITHOUT OVERTHINKING

➡️ **WHAT EMOTIONS ARISE WHEN I CONNECT WITH THIS CARD?**
Reflect on the energy of the card and how it resonates with your current journey

➡️ **HOW DOES THIS CARD'S MESSAGE APPLY TO MY LIFE TODAY?**
Explore how its wisdom can be integrated into your daily experience

➡️ **WHAT ACTIONS CAN I TAKE TO EMBODY THE ENERGY OF THIS CARD?**
List steps that align with the lesson or insight provided

➡️ **WHAT IS ONE AFFIRMATION I CAN CREATE FOR MYSELF BASED ON THIS CARD?**
Write your own empowering statement inspired by its meaning

➡️ **CREATIVE EXPRESSION**
(Space for drawing, doodling or writing additional thoughts related to the card)

➡️ **CLOSING INTENTION**
Write a short note of gratitude or intention for the day based on your reflections

➡️ **THANK THE TAROT, YOUR HIGHER SELF & THE UNIVERSE FOR GUIDANCE**

The Emperor

STABILITY, AUTHORITY, STRUCTURE AND LEADERSHIP

The Emperor's throne represents stability and solid foundations, while the rams adorning it symbolise strength, determination and assertive leadership.

I stand in my power, creating structure and stability in my life

Soul Journaling

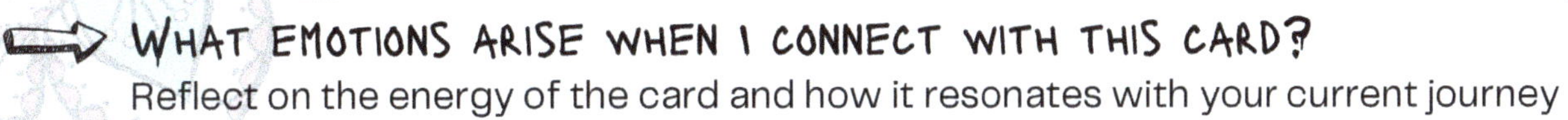

ALLOW YOUR SOUL TO SPEAK WITHOUT OVERTHINKING

⟹ **WHAT EMOTIONS ARISE WHEN I CONNECT WITH THIS CARD?**
Reflect on the energy of the card and how it resonates with your current journey

⟹ **HOW DOES THIS CARD'S MESSAGE APPLY TO MY LIFE TODAY?**
Explore how its wisdom can be integrated into your daily experience

⟹ **WHAT ACTIONS CAN I TAKE TO EMBODY THE ENERGY OF THIS CARD?**
List steps that align with the lesson or insight provided

⟹ **WHAT IS ONE AFFIRMATION I CAN CREATE FOR MYSELF BASED ON THIS CARD?**
Write your own empowering statement inspired by its meaning

⟹ **CREATIVE EXPRESSION**
(Space for drawing, doodling or writing additional thoughts related to the card)

⟹ **CLOSING INTENTION**
Write a short note of gratitude or intention for the day based on your reflections

⟹ **THANK THE TAROT, YOUR HIGHER SELF & THE UNIVERSE FOR GUIDANCE**

The Hierophant

TRADITION, SPIRITUAL TEACHINGS
AND SACRED WISDOM

The men at his feet represent devotion, tradition and the pursuit of spiritual knowledge. The Hierophant acts as a spiritual mentor, bridging the gap between the physical and the divine.

I honour spiritual wisdom and embrace divine guidance

Soul Journaling

➡ **WHAT EMOTIONS ARISE WHEN I CONNECT WITH THIS CARD?**
Reflect on the energy of the card and how it resonates with your current journey

➡ **HOW DOES THIS CARD'S MESSAGE APPLY TO MY LIFE TODAY?**
Explore how its wisdom can be integrated into your daily experience

➡ **WHAT ACTIONS CAN I TAKE TO EMBODY THE ENERGY OF THIS CARD?**
List steps that align with the lesson or insight provided

➡ **WHAT IS ONE AFFIRMATION I CAN CREATE FOR MYSELF BASED ON THIS CARD?**
Write your own empowering statement inspired by its meaning

➡ **CREATIVE EXPRESSION**
(Space for drawing, doodling or writing additional thoughts related to the card)

➡ **CLOSING INTENTION**
Write a short note of gratitude or intention for the day based on your reflections

➡ **THANK THE TAROT, YOUR HIGHER SELF & THE UNIVERSE FOR GUIDANCE**

The Lovers

RELATIONSHIPS, CHOICES
AND SOUL CONNECTIONS

The masculine and feminine energies reflect harmony and duality, with the angel above offering divine guidance. The mountain stands as a symbol of the deep spiritual bond they share.

I make choices that align with my highest good and deepest love

Soul Journaling

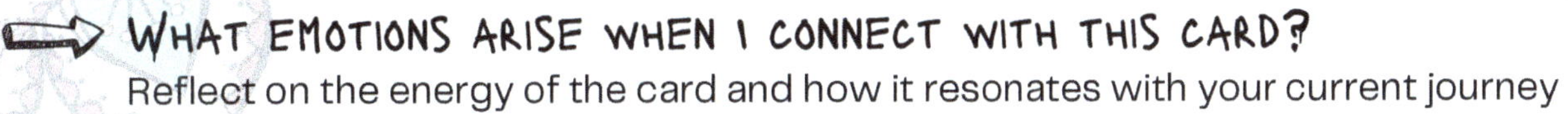

ALLOW YOUR SOUL TO SPEAK WITHOUT OVERTHINKING

⇨ **WHAT EMOTIONS ARISE WHEN I CONNECT WITH THIS CARD?**
Reflect on the energy of the card and how it resonates with your current journey

⇨ **HOW DOES THIS CARD'S MESSAGE APPLY TO MY LIFE TODAY?**
Explore how its wisdom can be integrated into your daily experience

⇨ **WHAT ACTIONS CAN I TAKE TO EMBODY THE ENERGY OF THIS CARD?**
List steps that align with the lesson or insight provided

⇨ **WHAT IS ONE AFFIRMATION I CAN CREATE FOR MYSELF BASED ON THIS CARD?**
Write your own empowering statement inspired by its meaning

⇨ **CREATIVE EXPRESSION**
(Space for drawing, doodling or writing additional thoughts related to the card)

⇨ **CLOSING INTENTION**
Write a short note of gratitude or intention for the day based on your reflections

⇨ **THANK THE TAROT, YOUR HIGHER SELF & THE UNIVERSE FOR GUIDANCE**

The Chariot

DETERMINATION, WILLPOWER
AND OVERCOMING OBSTACLES

The opposing sphinxes represent duality and balance, highlighting the need for direction.
The charioteer's armour signifies spiritual protection and strength as he moves forward.

I move forward with confidence and determination toward my dreams

Soul Journaling

ALLOW YOUR SOUL TO SPEAK WITHOUT OVERTHINKING

➡ **WHAT EMOTIONS ARISE WHEN I CONNECT WITH THIS CARD?**
Reflect on the energy of the card and how it resonates with your current journey

➡ **HOW DOES THIS CARD'S MESSAGE APPLY TO MY LIFE TODAY?**
Explore how its wisdom can be integrated into your daily experience

➡ **WHAT ACTIONS CAN I TAKE TO EMBODY THE ENERGY OF THIS CARD?**
List steps that align with the lesson or insight provided

➡ **WHAT IS ONE AFFIRMATION I CAN CREATE FOR MYSELF BASED ON THIS CARD?**
Write your own empowering statement inspired by its meaning

➡ **CREATIVE EXPRESSION**
(Space for drawing, doodling or writing additional thoughts related to the card)

➡ **CLOSING INTENTION**
Write a short note of gratitude or intention for the day based on your reflections

➡ **THANK THE TAROT, YOUR HIGHER SELF & THE UNIVERSE FOR GUIDANCE**

Strength

INNER STRENGTH, COURAGE
AND TAMING ONE'S EMOTIONS

The woman gently taming the lion represents inner strength and emotional mastery.
The infinity symbol above her head signifies infinite courage.

I embrace my inner strength with courage and compassion

Soul Journaling

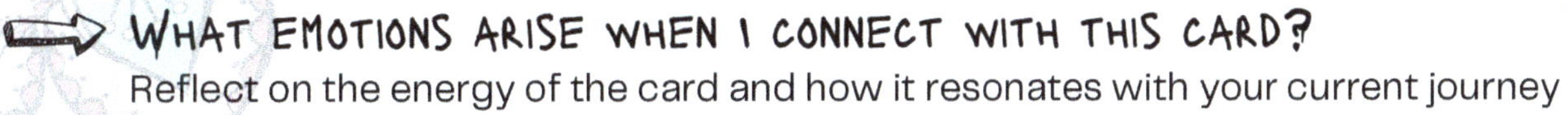

ALLOW YOUR SOUL TO SPEAK WITHOUT OVERTHINKING

➡ **WHAT EMOTIONS ARISE WHEN I CONNECT WITH THIS CARD?**
Reflect on the energy of the card and how it resonates with your current journey

➡ **HOW DOES THIS CARD'S MESSAGE APPLY TO MY LIFE TODAY?**
Explore how its wisdom can be integrated into your daily experience

➡ **WHAT ACTIONS CAN I TAKE TO EMBODY THE ENERGY OF THIS CARD?**
List steps that align with the lesson or insight provided

➡ **WHAT IS ONE AFFIRMATION I CAN CREATE FOR MYSELF BASED ON THIS CARD?**
Write your own empowering statement inspired by its meaning

➡ **CREATIVE EXPRESSION**
(Space for drawing, doodling or writing additional thoughts related to the card)

➡ **CLOSING INTENTION**
Write a short note of gratitude or intention for the day based on your reflections

➡ **THANK THE TAROT, YOUR HIGHER SELF & THE UNIVERSE FOR GUIDANCE**

The Hermit

SOLITUDE, INTROSPECTION
AND INNER WISDOM

His lantern symbolises inner light and the search for truth, illuminating the path of self-discovery. The staff represents wisdom gained through solitude and personal reflection, guiding him on his spiritual journey.

I find clarity and wisdom
within my solitude

Soul Journaling

ALLOW YOUR SOUL TO SPEAK WITHOUT OVERTHINKING

➡️ **WHAT EMOTIONS ARISE WHEN I CONNECT WITH THIS CARD?**
Reflect on the energy of the card and how it resonates with your current journey

➡️ **HOW DOES THIS CARD'S MESSAGE APPLY TO MY LIFE TODAY?**
Explore how its wisdom can be integrated into your daily experience

➡️ **WHAT ACTIONS CAN I TAKE TO EMBODY THE ENERGY OF THIS CARD?**
List steps that align with the lesson or insight provided

➡️ **WHAT IS ONE AFFIRMATION I CAN CREATE FOR MYSELF BASED ON THIS CARD?**
Write your own empowering statement inspired by its meaning

➡️ **CREATIVE EXPRESSION**
(Space for drawing, doodling or writing additional thoughts related to the card)

➡️ **CLOSING INTENTION**
Write a short note of gratitude or intention for the day based on your reflections

➡️ **THANK THE TAROT, YOUR HIGHER SELF & THE UNIVERSE FOR GUIDANCE**

Wheel of Fortune

FATE, CYCLES OF CHANGE
AND GOOD LUCK

The turning wheel symbolises the ever-changing cycles of life, fate and destiny, reminding us that nothing remains static. The figures surrounding it represent various spiritual forces at play, influencing the course of events and the unfolding of life's journey.

I trust the cycles of life
and welcome change with
an open heart

Soul Journaling

➡️ **WHAT EMOTIONS ARISE WHEN I CONNECT WITH THIS CARD?**
Reflect on the energy of the card and how it resonates with your current journey

➡️ **HOW DOES THIS CARD'S MESSAGE APPLY TO MY LIFE TODAY?**
Explore how its wisdom can be integrated into your daily experience

➡️ **WHAT ACTIONS CAN I TAKE TO EMBODY THE ENERGY OF THIS CARD?**
List steps that align with the lesson or insight provided

➡️ **WHAT IS ONE AFFIRMATION I CAN CREATE FOR MYSELF BASED ON THIS CARD?**
Write your own empowering statement inspired by its meaning

➡️ **CREATIVE EXPRESSION**
(Space for drawing, doodling or writing additional thoughts related to the card)

➡️ **CLOSING INTENTION**
Write a short note of gratitude or intention for the day based on your reflections

➡️ **THANK THE TAROT, YOUR HIGHER SELF & THE UNIVERSE FOR GUIDANCE**

Justice

FAIRNESS, TRUTH
AND KARMIC BALANCE

The scales symbolise balance, fairness and the pursuit of justice, ensuring that actions lead to rightful outcomes. The sword represents truth, clarity and decisiveness, cutting through illusion to reveal integrity and accountability.

I stand in my truth and trust
in divine fairness and balance

Soul Journaling

➡ **WHAT EMOTIONS ARISE WHEN I CONNECT WITH THIS CARD?**
Reflect on the energy of the card and how it resonates with your current journey

➡ **HOW DOES THIS CARD'S MESSAGE APPLY TO MY LIFE TODAY?**
Explore how its wisdom can be integrated into your daily experience

➡ **WHAT ACTIONS CAN I TAKE TO EMBODY THE ENERGY OF THIS CARD?**
List steps that align with the lesson or insight provided

➡ **WHAT IS ONE AFFIRMATION I CAN CREATE FOR MYSELF BASED ON THIS CARD?**
Write your own empowering statement inspired by its meaning

➡ **CREATIVE EXPRESSION**
(Space for drawing, doodling or writing additional thoughts related to the card)

➡ **CLOSING INTENTION**
Write a short note of gratitude or intention for the day based on your reflections

➡ **THANK THE TAROT, YOUR HIGHER SELF & THE UNIVERSE FOR GUIDANCE**

The Hanged Man

SURRENDER, PERSPECTIVE SHIFT AND PATIENCE

The upside-down position symbolises a shift in perspective and the need for surrender, encouraging a new way of seeing the world. The glowing halo represents spiritual enlightenment and higher wisdom, gained through patience and introspection.

I surrender to divine timing and see life from a new perspective

Soul Journaling

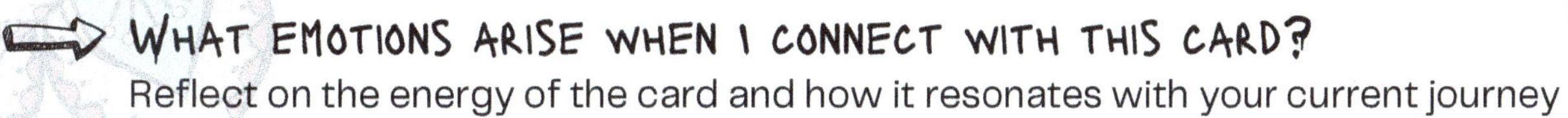

ALLOW YOUR SOUL TO SPEAK WITHOUT OVERTHINKING

⟹ **WHAT EMOTIONS ARISE WHEN I CONNECT WITH THIS CARD?**
Reflect on the energy of the card and how it resonates with your current journey

⟹ **HOW DOES THIS CARD'S MESSAGE APPLY TO MY LIFE TODAY?**
Explore how its wisdom can be integrated into your daily experience

⟹ **WHAT ACTIONS CAN I TAKE TO EMBODY THE ENERGY OF THIS CARD?**
List steps that align with the lesson or insight provided

⟹ **WHAT IS ONE AFFIRMATION I CAN CREATE FOR MYSELF BASED ON THIS CARD?**
Write your own empowering statement inspired by its meaning

⟹ **CREATIVE EXPRESSION**
(Space for drawing, doodling or writing additional thoughts related to the card)

⟹ **CLOSING INTENTION**
Write a short note of gratitude or intention for the day based on your reflections

⟹ **THANK THE TAROT, YOUR HIGHER SELF & THE UNIVERSE FOR GUIDANCE**

Death

TRANSFORMATION, ENDINGS
AND NEW BEGINNINGS

The skeleton symbolises profound transformation, the shedding of the old to make way for the new, reminding us that change is an essential part of growth. The rising sun in the background signifies rebirth, renewal and the promise of new beginnings after endings.

AFFIRMATION

I release the old to welcome powerful transformation and rebirth

Soul Journaling

➡ **WHAT EMOTIONS ARISE WHEN I CONNECT WITH THIS CARD?**
Reflect on the energy of the card and how it resonates with your current journey

➡ **HOW DOES THIS CARD'S MESSAGE APPLY TO MY LIFE TODAY?**
Explore how its wisdom can be integrated into your daily experience

➡ **WHAT ACTIONS CAN I TAKE TO EMBODY THE ENERGY OF THIS CARD?**
List steps that align with the lesson or insight provided

➡ **WHAT IS ONE AFFIRMATION I CAN CREATE FOR MYSELF BASED ON THIS CARD?**
Write your own empowering statement inspired by its meaning

➡ **CREATIVE EXPRESSION**
(Space for drawing, doodling or writing additional thoughts related to the card)

➡ **CLOSING INTENTION**
Write a short note of gratitude or intention for the day based on your reflections

➡ **THANK THE TAROT, YOUR HIGHER SELF & THE UNIVERSE FOR GUIDANCE**

Temperance

BALANCE, MODERATION
AND SPIRITUAL ALCHEMY

The angel gracefully transfers water between two cups, symbolising the continuous flow of energy, the integration of opposites and the pursuit of balance. This action reflects harmony, patience and the importance of equilibrium in all areas of life.

I find harmony and balance
in all aspects of my life

Soul Journaling

➡ **WHAT EMOTIONS ARISE WHEN I CONNECT WITH THIS CARD?**
Reflect on the energy of the card and how it resonates with your current journey

➡ **HOW DOES THIS CARD'S MESSAGE APPLY TO MY LIFE TODAY?**
Explore how its wisdom can be integrated into your daily experience

➡ **WHAT ACTIONS CAN I TAKE TO EMBODY THE ENERGY OF THIS CARD?**
List steps that align with the lesson or insight provided

➡ **WHAT IS ONE AFFIRMATION I CAN CREATE FOR MYSELF BASED ON THIS CARD?**
Write your own empowering statement inspired by its meaning

➡ **CREATIVE EXPRESSION**
(Space for drawing, doodling or writing additional thoughts related to the card)

➡ **CLOSING INTENTION**
Write a short note of gratitude or intention for the day based on your reflections

➡ **THANK THE TAROT, YOUR HIGHER SELF & THE UNIVERSE FOR GUIDANCE**

The Devil

TEMPTATION, MATERIALISM
AND BREAKING FREE FROM TOXIC PATTERNS

The chained figures symbolise bondage to addiction, unhealthy attachments, and dependency. The Devil represents illusion, material temptation and the darker aspects of human desire, reminding us to recognise and break free from what no longer serves us.

I free myself from limiting beliefs and embrace my true power

Soul Journaling

ALLOW YOUR SOUL TO SPEAK WITHOUT OVERTHINKING

➡ **WHAT EMOTIONS ARISE WHEN I CONNECT WITH THIS CARD?**
Reflect on the energy of the card and how it resonates with your current journey

➡ **HOW DOES THIS CARD'S MESSAGE APPLY TO MY LIFE TODAY?**
Explore how its wisdom can be integrated into your daily experience

➡ **WHAT ACTIONS CAN I TAKE TO EMBODY THE ENERGY OF THIS CARD?**
List steps that align with the lesson or insight provided

➡ **WHAT IS ONE AFFIRMATION I CAN CREATE FOR MYSELF BASED ON THIS CARD?**
Write your own empowering statement inspired by its meaning

➡ **CREATIVE EXPRESSION**
(Space for drawing, doodling or writing additional thoughts related to the card)

➡ **CLOSING INTENTION**
Write a short note of gratitude or intention for the day based on your reflections

➡ **THANK THE TAROT, YOUR HIGHER SELF & THE UNIVERSE FOR GUIDANCE**

The Tower

SUDDEN CHANGE, UPHEAVAL
AND BREAKING DOWN ILLUSIONS

A bolt of lightning crashes down, symbolising sudden upheaval, unexpected change and the breaking down of false foundations. This powerful force represents a necessary transformation, clearing the way for truth, growth and new beginnings.

I welcome change and trust that destruction leads to new beginnings

Soul Journaling

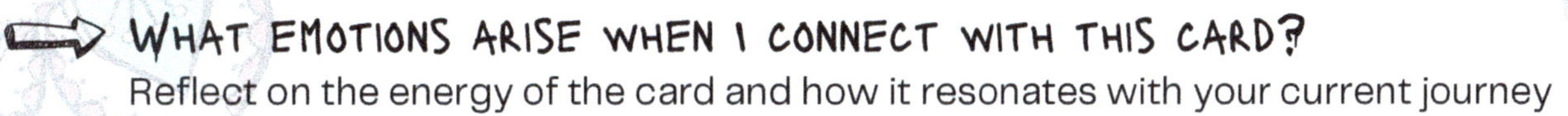

ALLOW YOUR SOUL TO SPEAK WITHOUT OVERTHINKING

➡ **WHAT EMOTIONS ARISE WHEN I CONNECT WITH THIS CARD?**
Reflect on the energy of the card and how it resonates with your current journey

➡ **HOW DOES THIS CARD'S MESSAGE APPLY TO MY LIFE TODAY?**
Explore how its wisdom can be integrated into your daily experience

➡ **WHAT ACTIONS CAN I TAKE TO EMBODY THE ENERGY OF THIS CARD?**
List steps that align with the lesson or insight provided

➡ **WHAT IS ONE AFFIRMATION I CAN CREATE FOR MYSELF BASED ON THIS CARD?**
Write your own empowering statement inspired by its meaning

➡ **CREATIVE EXPRESSION**
(Space for drawing, doodling or writing additional thoughts related to the card)

➡ **CLOSING INTENTION**
Write a short note of gratitude or intention for the day based on your reflections

➡ **THANK THE TAROT, YOUR HIGHER SELF & THE UNIVERSE FOR GUIDANCE**

The Star

HOPE, INSPIRATION
AND DIVINE GUIDANCE

The flowing water represents renewal, healing and the continuous cycle of spiritual growth, cleansing the past and making way for new possibilities. The star is a guiding light of hope, inspiration and reassurance, reminding us to trust in the universe and our path forward.

AFFIRMATION

I am guided by divine light
and infinite hope

Soul Journaling

ALLOW YOUR SOUL TO SPEAK WITHOUT OVERTHINKING

➡️ **WHAT EMOTIONS ARISE WHEN I CONNECT WITH THIS CARD?**
Reflect on the energy of the card and how it resonates with your current journey

➡️ **HOW DOES THIS CARD'S MESSAGE APPLY TO MY LIFE TODAY?**
Explore how its wisdom can be integrated into your daily experience

➡️ **WHAT ACTIONS CAN I TAKE TO EMBODY THE ENERGY OF THIS CARD?**
List steps that align with the lesson or insight provided

➡️ **WHAT IS ONE AFFIRMATION I CAN CREATE FOR MYSELF BASED ON THIS CARD?**
Write your own empowering statement inspired by its meaning

➡️ **CREATIVE EXPRESSION**
(Space for drawing, doodling or writing additional thoughts related to the card)

➡️ **CLOSING INTENTION**
Write a short note of gratitude or intention for the day based on your reflections

➡️ **THANK THE TAROT, YOUR HIGHER SELF & THE UNIVERSE FOR GUIDANCE**

The Moon

ILLUSIONS, INTUITION
AND SUBCONSCIOUS FEARS

The winding path between the two towers represents the journey into the unknown, where uncertainty unfold. The moon symbolises intuition and dreams, reminding us to trust our inner wisdom while navigating the hidden depths of our subconscious.

AFFIRMATION

I embrace my shadows and trust the wisdom of my subconscious

Soul Journaling

ALLOW YOUR SOUL TO SPEAK WITHOUT OVERTHINKING

➡️ **WHAT EMOTIONS ARISE WHEN I CONNECT WITH THIS CARD?**
Reflect on the energy of the card and how it resonates with your current journey

➡️ **HOW DOES THIS CARD'S MESSAGE APPLY TO MY LIFE TODAY?**
Explore how its wisdom can be integrated into your daily experience

➡️ **WHAT ACTIONS CAN I TAKE TO EMBODY THE ENERGY OF THIS CARD?**
List steps that align with the lesson or insight provided

➡️ **WHAT IS ONE AFFIRMATION I CAN CREATE FOR MYSELF BASED ON THIS CARD?**
Write your own empowering statement inspired by its meaning

➡️ **CREATIVE EXPRESSION**
(Space for drawing, doodling or writing additional thoughts related to the card)

➡️ **CLOSING INTENTION**
Write a short note of gratitude or intention for the day based on your reflections

➡️ **THANK THE TAROT, YOUR HIGHER SELF & THE UNIVERSE FOR GUIDANCE**

The Sun

JOY, CLARITY
AND SUCCESS

The radiant sun shines brightly, symbolising vitality, enlightenment and the power of clarity and truth. The child riding forward with open arms represents pure joy, innocence and the freedom that comes from embracing life with optimism and authenticity.

I radiate joy, vitality and positivity in all that I do

Soul Journaling

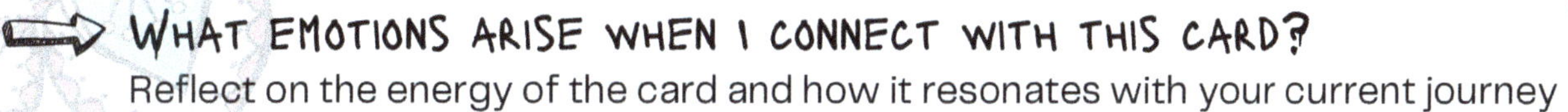

ALLOW YOUR SOUL TO SPEAK WITHOUT OVERTHINKING

⇨ **WHAT EMOTIONS ARISE WHEN I CONNECT WITH THIS CARD?**
Reflect on the energy of the card and how it resonates with your current journey

⇨ **HOW DOES THIS CARD'S MESSAGE APPLY TO MY LIFE TODAY?**
Explore how its wisdom can be integrated into your daily experience

⇨ **WHAT ACTIONS CAN I TAKE TO EMBODY THE ENERGY OF THIS CARD?**
List steps that align with the lesson or insight provided

⇨ **WHAT IS ONE AFFIRMATION I CAN CREATE FOR MYSELF BASED ON THIS CARD?**
Write your own empowering statement inspired by its meaning

⇨ **CREATIVE EXPRESSION**
(Space for drawing, doodling or writing additional thoughts related to the card)

⇨ **CLOSING INTENTION**
Write a short note of gratitude or intention for the day based on your reflections

⇨ **THANK THE TAROT, YOUR HIGHER SELF & THE UNIVERSE FOR GUIDANCE**

Judgement

AWAKENING, SELF-REFLECTION
AND HIGHER CALLING

The angel's trumpet sounds a divine call to awakening, signaling a time of profound transformation. This celestial sound represents spiritual renewal, self-reflection and the opportunity to rise above the past into a new phase of enlightenment and purpose.

I awaken to my soul's purpose and embrace my higher calling

Soul Journaling

➡️ **WHAT EMOTIONS ARISE WHEN I CONNECT WITH THIS CARD?**
Reflect on the energy of the card and how it resonates with your current journey

➡️ **HOW DOES THIS CARD'S MESSAGE APPLY TO MY LIFE TODAY?**
Explore how its wisdom can be integrated into your daily experience

➡️ **WHAT ACTIONS CAN I TAKE TO EMBODY THE ENERGY OF THIS CARD?**
List steps that align with the lesson or insight provided

➡️ **WHAT IS ONE AFFIRMATION I CAN CREATE FOR MYSELF BASED ON THIS CARD?**
Write your own empowering statement inspired by its meaning

➡️ **CREATIVE EXPRESSION**
(Space for drawing, doodling or writing additional thoughts related to the card)

➡️ **CLOSING INTENTION**
Write a short note of gratitude or intention for the day based on your reflections

➡️ **THANK THE TAROT, YOUR HIGHER SELF & THE UNIVERSE FOR GUIDANCE**

The World

COMPLETION, WHOLENESS
AND FULFILMENT

The laurel wreath encircles the central figure, symbolising wholeness, achievement and the fulfilment of a significant journey. It represents completion, victory and the harmony that comes from reaching a state of balance and enlightenment.

I celebrate my journey and embrace the wholeness of my being

Soul Journaling

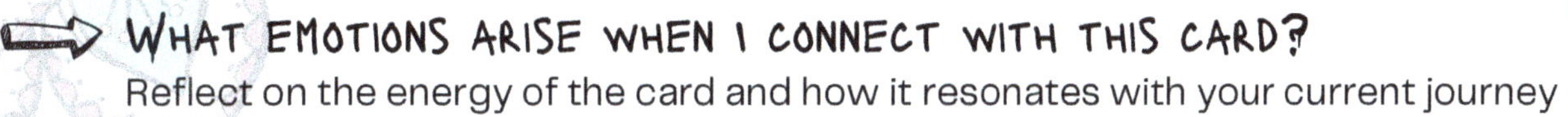

ALLOW YOUR SOUL TO SPEAK WITHOUT OVERTHINKING

⇨ **WHAT EMOTIONS ARISE WHEN I CONNECT WITH THIS CARD?**
Reflect on the energy of the card and how it resonates with your current journey

⇨ **HOW DOES THIS CARD'S MESSAGE APPLY TO MY LIFE TODAY?**
Explore how its wisdom can be integrated into your daily experience

⇨ **WHAT ACTIONS CAN I TAKE TO EMBODY THE ENERGY OF THIS CARD?**
List steps that align with the lesson or insight provided

⇨ **WHAT IS ONE AFFIRMATION I CAN CREATE FOR MYSELF BASED ON THIS CARD?**
Write your own empowering statement inspired by its meaning

⇨ **CREATIVE EXPRESSION**
(Space for drawing, doodling or writing additional thoughts related to the card)

⇨ **CLOSING INTENTION**
Write a short note of gratitude or intention for the day based on your reflections

⇨ **THANK THE TAROT, YOUR HIGHER SELF & THE UNIVERSE FOR GUIDANCE**

Notes

Notes

Thank you for walking this path with me through The Tarot Journey. I hope this book has brought you insight, inspiration and a deeper connection to yourself and the wisdom of the Tarot.

Every card you draw, every affirmation you speak and every moment of reflection is part of your unfolding story. Trust the journey, embrace the lessons and honour the magic within you.

I am deeply grateful for your time, energy and presence. If this book has resonated with you, I would love to hear about your experience. Your reflections and shared insights mean the world to me.

May your journey continue, unfolding with wisdom, love and light.

PUBLISHED WORLDWIDE

MMXXV

ISBN 978-1-7640433-0-4

9 781764 043304 >